A NOT-SO-SCARY MONSTER!

Jonathan Fenske

Scholastic Inc.

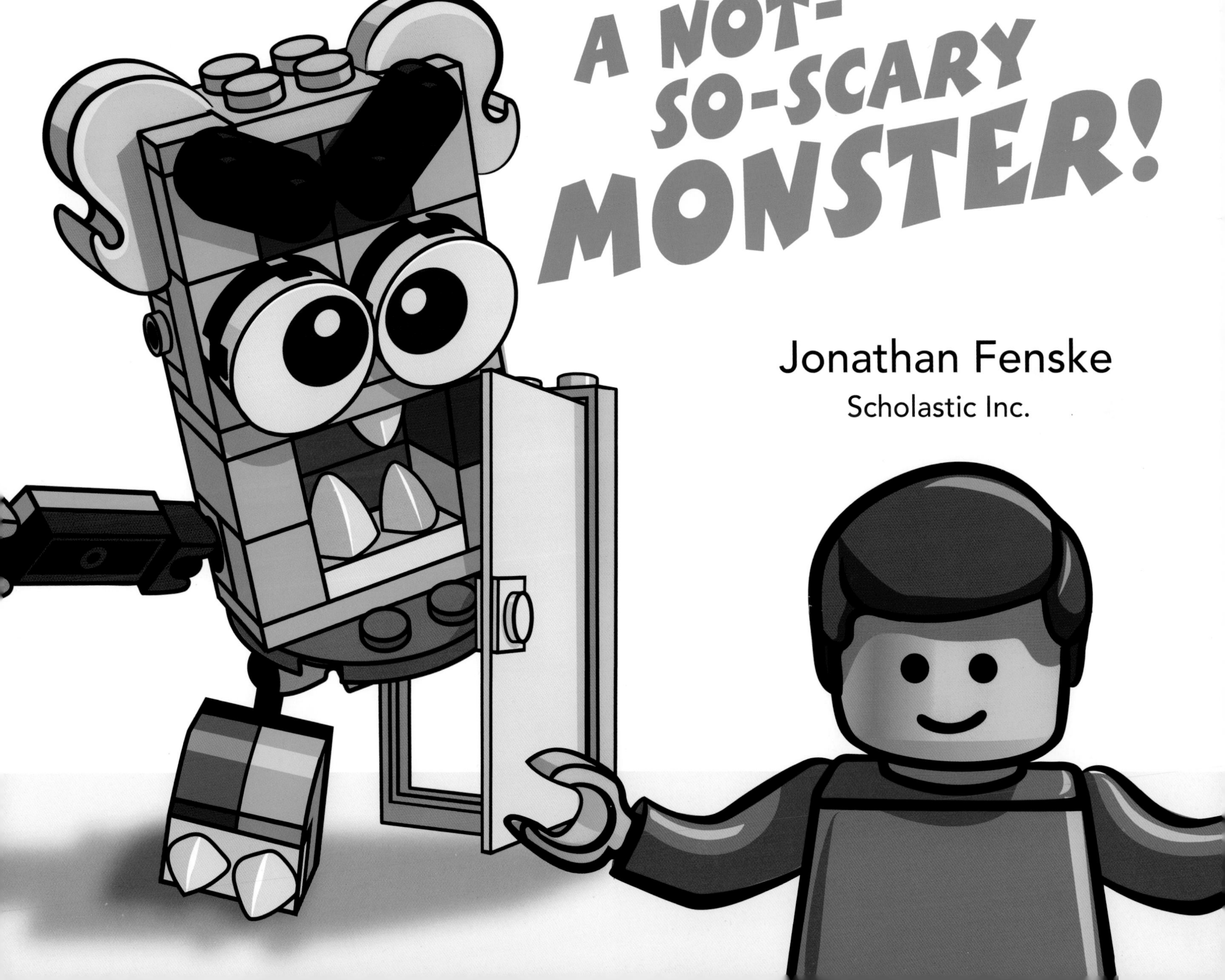

ISBN 978-1-338-36082-0

10 9 8 7 6 5 4 3 2 1 20 21 22 23 24

Printed in China 62

First edition 2020

BOO!

EEEK!

You scared the pants off me!

I'm sorry.
That's okay.
You are a monster.
Monsters are meant
to be SCARY.

I know.
But guess what?

Are you going to take me apart ?
No, silly!

Phew.

It's just—
sometimes
I don't WANT
to be scary.

Sometimes you don't want to be scary?
I know, I know. I am an embarrassment to monsters everywhere.

Have you tried to NOT be scary?
I am a MONSTER. I can't NOT be scary!
I see. So you are a scary monster who is scared to not be scary.
Exactly.
Wait. Huh?

It is true.
You ARE a monster.
Don’t remind me.

But it is NOT true that you always have to be scary.
Really?

Yes! You can be any kind of monster you want to be!

Do you mean it?

You are a MONSTER.
Who is going to stop you?
You make a
good point.

So, if I'm feeling happy,
I can be a happy monster?

You sure can!

And if I'm feeling sad, I can be a sad monster?

Awww. Of course.

And if I'm feeling grumpy, I can be a grumpy monster?

Uh, I think you are putting it all together.

Blugga, blurga, bloop!
Guess who is feeling like a SILLY monster?!

Hmmm...
I wonder who
that could be?

Meeeeeeeeee!

Now where did that monster go?

BOO!
EEEK!

Can I still be scary sometimes?
Sigh. If you really must.
Yay!
Guess what?
Are you going to take me apart NOW?
How did you know?
GULP!

Hee, hee!
Just kidding!

See? I can be a FUNNY monster, too!

Now I've REALLY created a monster.